21 Lovely Lullabies
with Wonderful Works of Art

Kumato George

21 Lovely Lullabies with Wonderful Works of Art

Edited by
Kumato George

Curation, layout, and design by Kumato George

This is a collection of works individually available in the public domain. The layout and arrangement of these works is protected by copyright as the collection contained herein.

ISBN-13: 978-1987415094
ISBN-10: 1987415094

Contents

The Alphabet Song

All the Pretty Horses

All Through the Night

Amazing Grace

Ba Ba Black Sheep

Brahm's Lullaby

Day is Done

Emmet's Lullaby

Frère Jacques

Golden Slumber

Hush, Little Baby

Itsy-Bitsy Spider

Lavender's Blue

Little Boy Blue

Mary Had Little Lamb

Rock-a-Bye Baby

Sleep, Baby, Sleep

Swing Low, Sweet Chariot

Too Ra Loo Ra Loo Ral

Twinkle, Twinkle, Little Star

Winkum, Winkum

The Alphabet Song

A B C D E F G
H I J K L M N O P
Q R S , T U V
W X, Y and Z

Now I know my ABC's
Next time won't you sing with me

All the Pretty Horses

Hush-a-bye, don't you cry,
Go to sleep my little baby.
When you wake you shall have
All the pretty little horses.
Black and bays, dapples, grays,
All the pretty little horses.
Hush-a-bye, don't you cry,
Go to sleep my little baby.
Hush-a-bye, don't you cry,
Go to sleep my little baby.
When you wake you shall have
All the pretty little horses.

All Through the Night

Sleep, my child, and peace attend thee,
All through the night
Guardian angels God will send thee,
All through the night
Soft the drowsy hours are creeping,
Hill and dale in slumber sleeping
I my loved ones' watch am keeping,
All through the night
Angels watching, e'er around thee,
All through the night
Midnight slumber close surround thee,
All through the night
Soft the drowsy hours are creeping,
Hill and dale in slumber sleeping
I my loved ones' watch am keeping,
All through the night

Amazing Grace

Amazing grace! How sweet the sound
That saved a wretch like me
I once was lost but now am found
Was blind but now I see

'Twas grace that taught my heart to fear
And grace my fears relieved
How precious did that grace appear
The hour I first believed

Through many dangers, toils and snares
I have already come
'Tis grace hath brought me safe thus far
And grace will lead me home

How sweet the name of Jesus sounds
In a believer's ear
It soothes his sorrows, heals his wounds
And drives away his fear

Must Jesus bear the cross alone
And all the world go free?
No, there's a cross for everyone
And there's a cross for me

Baa Baa Black Sheep

Baa, baa, black sheep,
Have you any wool?
Yes, sir, yes, sir,
Three bags full;
One for the master,
And one for the dame,
And one for the little boy
Who lives down the lane.

Brahm's Lullaby
(Lullaby and Goodnight)

Lullaby and goodnight, with roses bedight
With lilies o'er spread is baby's wee bed
Lay thee down now and rest, may thy slumber be
blessed
Lay thee down now and rest, may thy slumber be
blessed

Lullaby and goodnight, thy mother's delight
Bright angels beside my darling abide
They will guard thee at rest, thou shalt wake on my
breast
They will guard thee at rest, thou shalt wake on my
breast

Day is Done

Day is done,
Gone the sun,
From the lake, from the hills, from the sky.
All is well, safely rest,
God is nigh.

Emmett's Lullaby
(Go to Sleep, Lena Darling)

Close your eyes, Lena, my darling,
While I sing your lullaby;
Fear thou no danger, Lena,
Move not, dear Lena, my darling;
For your brother watches nigh you, Lena dear.
Angels guide thee, Lena dear, my darling,
Nothing evil can come near;
Brightest flowers bloom for thee,
Darling Lena, dear to me.

Go to sleep, go to sleep, my baby,
My baby, my baby.
Go to sleep, my baby, baby, oh! by,
Go to sleep, Lena, sleep.
Bright be the morning, my darling,
When you ope your eyes,
Sunbeams grow all around you, Lena,
Peace be with thee, love, my darling;
Blue and cloudless be the sky for Lena dear,
Birds sing their bright songs for thee, my darling,
Full of sweetest melody;
Angels ever hover near,
Darling Lena, dear to me.

Frère Jacques (Are You Sleeping?)

Frère Jacques, Frère Jacques,
Dormez-vous? Dormez-vous?
Sonnez les matines, sonnez les matines
Ding ding dong, ding ding dong.

English version
Are you sleeping, are you sleeping?
Brother John, Brother John?
Morning bells are ringing, morning bells are ringing
Ding ding dong, ding ding dong.

Golden Slumbers

Golden slumbers kiss your eyes,
Smiles await you when you rise.
Sleep,
Pretty baby,
Do not cry,
And I will sing a lullaby.

Cares you know not,
Therefore sleep,
While over you a watch I'll keep.
Sleep,
Pretty darling,
Do not cry,
And I will sing a lullaby.

Hush, Little Baby

Hush, little baby, don't say a word.
Papa's gonna buy you a mockingbird

And if that mockingbird won't sing,
Papa's gonna buy you a diamond ring

And if that diamond ring turns brass,
Papa's gonna buy you a looking glass

And if that looking glass gets broke,
Papa's gonna buy you a billy goat

And if that billy goat won't pull,
Papa's gonna buy you a cart and bull

And if that cart and bull turn over,
Papa's gonna buy you a dog named Rover

And if that dog named Rover won't bark
Papa's gonna buy you a horse and cart

And if that horse and cart fall down,
You'll still be the sweetest little baby in town.

Itsy-Bitsy Spider

The itsy-bitsy spider
Climbed up the water spout
Down came the rain
And washed the spider out
Out came the sun
And dried up all the rain
And the itsy-bitsy spider
Climbed up the spout again

Lavender's Blue

Lavender's blue, dilly, dilly, lavender's green,
When I am king, dilly, dilly, You shall be queen.
Who told you so, dilly, dilly, who told you so?
'Twas my own heart, dilly, dilly, that told me so.

Call up your men, dilly, dilly, set them to work,
Some to the plough, dilly, dilly, some to the fork.
Some to make hay, dilly, dilly, some to cut corn,
While you and I, dilly, dilly, keep ourselves warm.

Lavender's green, dilly, dilly, Lavender's blue,
if you love me, dilly, dilly, I will love you.
Let the birds sing, dilly, dilly, And the lambs play,
We shall be safe, dilly, dilly, out of harm's way.

I love to dance, dilly, dilly, I love to sing,
When I am queen, dilly, dilly, You'll be my king.
Who told me so, dilly, dilly, Who told me so?
I told myself, dilly, dilly, I told me so.

Little Boy Blue

Little boy blue, come blow your horn,
The sheep's in the meadow, the cow's in the corn
Where is the boy who looks after the sheep?
He's under the haystack, fast asleep.

Mary Had A Little Lamb

Mary had a little lamb,
His fleece was white as snow,
And everywhere that Mary went,
The lamb was sure to go.

He followed her to school one day,
Which was against the rule,
It made the children laugh and play
To see a lamb at school.

And so the teacher turned it out,
But still it lingered near,
And waited patiently about,
Till Mary did appear.

"Why does the lamb love Mary so?"
The eager children cry.
"Why, Mary loves the lamb, you know,"
The teacher did reply.

Rock-A-Bye Baby

Rock-a-bye baby, in the treetop
When the wind blows, the cradle will rock
When the bough breaks, the cradle will fall
And down will come baby, cradle and all

Sleep, Baby, Sleep

Sleep, baby, sleep
Your father tends the sheep
Your mother shakes the dreamland tree
And from it fall sweet dreams for thee
Sleep, baby, sleep
Sleep, baby, sleep

Sleep, baby, sleep
Our cottage vale is deep
The little lamb is on the green
With snowy fleece so soft and clean
Sleep, baby, sleep
Sleep, baby, sleep

Swing Low, Sweet Chariot

Swing low, sweet chariot
Comin' for to carry me home
Swing low, sweet chariot
Comin' for to carry me home

I looked over Jordan and what did
I see
Comin' for to carry me home
A band of angels comin' after me
Comin' for to carry me home

Swing low, sweet chariot
Comin' for to carry me home
Swing low, sweet chariot
Comin' for to carry me home

If you get to heaven before I do
Comin' for to carry me home
Tell all my friends I'm comin' there
too
Comin' for to carry me home

Swing low, sweet chariot
Comin' for to carry me home
Swing low, sweet chariot
Comin' for to carry me home

I'm sometimes up and sometimes
down
Comin' for to carry me home
But still I know I'm heavenly
(freedom) bound
Comin' for to carry me home

Swing low, sweet chariot
Comin' for to carry me home
Swing low, sweet chariot
Comin' for to carry me home

If I get there before you do
Comin' for to carry me home
I'll cut a hole and pull you through
Comin' for to carry me home

Swing low, sweet chariot
Comin' for to carry me home
Swing low, sweet chariot
Comin' for to carry me home

Too Ra Loo Ra Loo Ral
(That's an Irish Lullaby)

Over in Killarney, many years ago
Me Mother sang a song to me, in tones so sweet and low.
Just a simple little ditty, in her good old Irish way,
And I'd give the world if she could sing, that song to me
this day.

Too-ra-loo-ra-loo-ral,
Too-ra-loo-ra-li,
Too-ra-loo-ra-loo-ral,
Hush now don't you cry!
Too-ra-loo-ra-loo-ral,
Too-ra-loo-ra-li,
Too-ra-loo-ra-loo-ral,
That's an Irish lullaby.

Oft, in dreams I wander, to that cot again,
I feel her arms a huggin' me, as when she held me then.
And I hear her voice a hummin', to me as in days of yore,
When she used to rock me fast asleep, outside the cabin
door.

Twinkle Twinkle Little Star

Twinkle, twinkle, little star
How I wonder what you are!
Up above the world so high
Like a diamond in the sky
Twinkle, twinkle, little star
How I wonder what you are

Winkum, Winkum

Winkum, winkum, shut your eye,
Sweet, my baby, lullaby,
For the dew is falling soft,
Lights are flickering up aloft.
And the moonlight's peeping over,
Yonder hill top capped with clover.

Chickens long have gone to rest,
Birds lie snug within their nest,
And my birdie soon will be
Sleeping like a chick-a-dee.
For with only half a try,
Winkum, winkum, shuts her eye.

Artwork

The Alphabet Song: *Musical Group on a Balcony* by Gerrit van Honthorst

All the Pretty Horses: *The Piebald Horse* by Paulus Potter

All Through the Night: *A Walk at Dusk* by Caspar David Friedrich

Amazing Grace: *Immaculate Conception* by Placido Costanzi

Ba Ba Black Sheep: *Shepherd and Sleeping Shepherdess* by Reyer Jacobsz van Blommendael

Brahm's Lullaby: *The Russian Cradle* by Jean-Baptiste Le Prince

Day is Done: *Landscape with Lake and Boatman* by Jean-Baptiste-Camille Corot

Emmet's Lullaby: *Irises* by Vincent van Gogh

Frère Jacques: *Saint Francis and a Bishop Saint* by Fra Angelico

Golden Slumber: *Penelope Unraveling Her Web* by Joseph Wright

Hush, Little Baby: *The Birds Catchers* by Francois Boucher

Itsy-Bitsy Spider: *The Holy Family* by Raffaello Sanzio

Lavender's Blue: *A Centennial of Independence* by Henri Rousseau

Little Boy Blue: *Wheatstacks, Snow Effect, Morning* by Claude Monet

Mary Had Little Lamb: *The Fountain of Love* by Francois Boucher

Rock-a-Bye Baby: *Study of Clouds with a Sunset near Rome* by Simon Alexandre Clément Denis

Sleep, Baby, Sleep: *Adoration of the Shepherds* by Nicolaes Maes

Swing Low, Sweet Chariot: *Four Studies of a Male Head* by Peter Paul Rubens

Too Ra Loo Ra Loo Ral: *Head of a Woman* by Michael Sweerts

Twinkle, Twinkle, Little Star: *Starry Night Over the Rhone* by Vincent van Gogh

Winkum, Winkum: *The Adoration of the Shepherds* by Sebastiano Conca

Cover: *The Wounded Foot* by Joaquin Sorolla y Bastida

Back Cover: *Jeanne (Spring)* by Edouard Manet

Contents: *A Hare in the Forest* by Hans Hoffmann

Artwork index: *La Promenade* by Pierre-Auguste Renoir

Made in the USA
Monee, IL
28 October 2020